To Gracie—

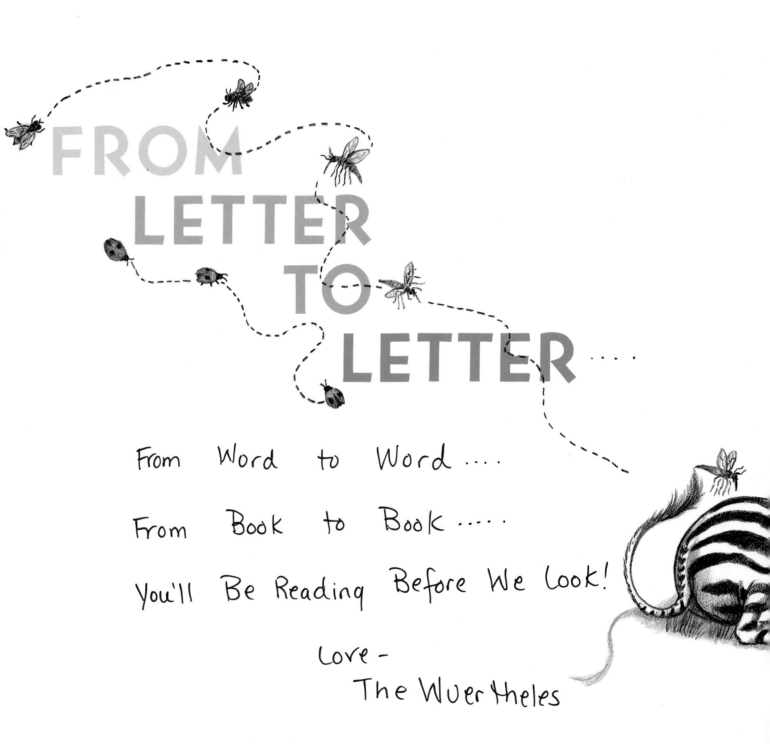

FROM
LETTER
TO
LETTER

From Word to Word....

From Book to Book.....

You'll Be Reading Before We Look!

Love—
The Wuertheles

FROM
LETTER
TO
LETTER

Teri Sloat

A Puffin Unicorn

astronaut · airplane · acorn · apple · ant · alphabet · alligator · armadillo · ark · anchor · anthill ·

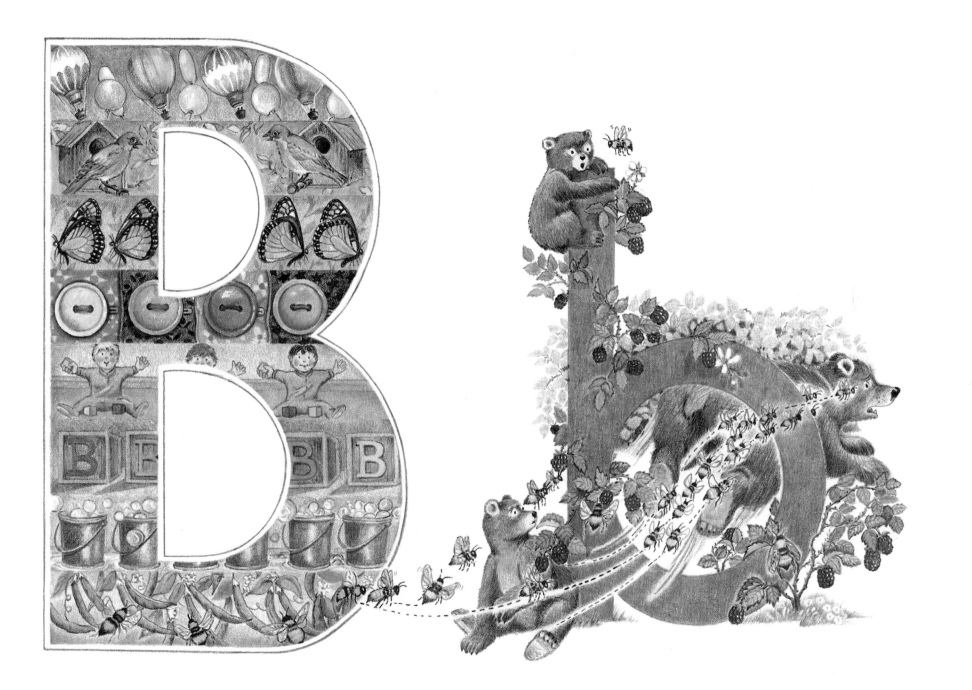

balloon · bluebird · butterfly · button · baby · block · bucket · bubble · bean · blossom · bee · bear ·

Look at the back of the book for more words for the pictures.

cherry · crayon · candy cane · cupcake · candle · castle · Christmas cookie · camel · clown · carrot ·

dinosaur · doll · drum · drumstick · domino · dice · deer · dog · daffodil · daisy · dolphin · dandelion ·

elephant · eight · eleven · eighteen · echidna · eagle · egg · eye · eggplant · ermine · Eskimo · elf ·

flag · fruit · flashlight · forest · fox · flamingo · frog · fish · fly · fiddler · fiddle · flute · farmer · flower ·

goldfish · grasshopper · gumball · gorilla · goat · goose · garden · gopher · gumdrop · gingerbread ·

hen · hive · honeybee · hat · hydrant · hopscotch · hose · holly · hamburger · hedgehog · hippopotamus ·

ice-cream cone · ice cube · iron · ironing board · inchworm · inch · impala · iguana · ink bottle · ink ·

jet · jack · joker · jump rope · jack-o'-lantern · jelly bean · jewelry · jack-in-the-box · jacks · jellyfish ·

kite · koala · kitten · knot · keyboard · key · keyhole · kid · kangaroo · kiwi · karate · kick · kung fu ·

lighthouse · lobster · lollipop · loon · lily · lion · lemon · ladder · library · librarian · light · leak · lock ·

moon · mountain · match · music · marble · mouse · mushroom · mole · magician · magic wand · mop ·

nuthatch · nest · nut · nail · nothing · notebook · needle · narwhal · nutcracker · newspaper · needlework ·

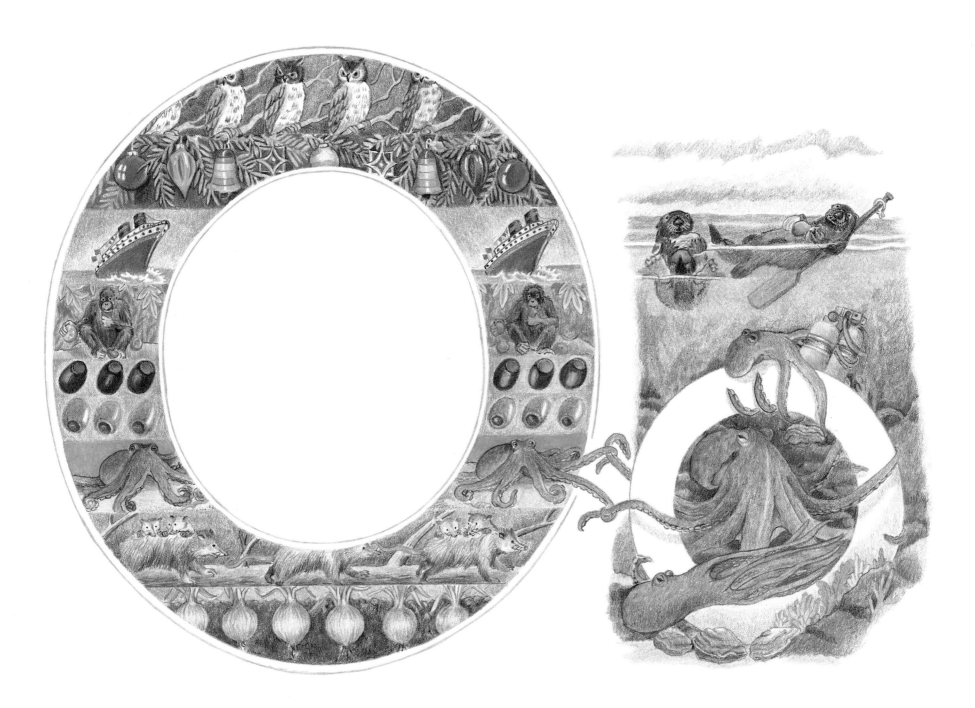

owl · ornament · ocean liner · orangutan · olive · octopus · opossum · onion · ocean · otter · oar ·

pear · peach · pig · penguin · pea · porcupine · paint · popcorn · pumpkin · parade · paddle · people ·

Quonset hut · quadruplet · quill · quail · question · quince · queue · quilt · queen · quicksand · quetzal ·

rainbow · rain · robin · raccoon · rat · rope · ring · ribbon · rose · rabbit · radish · rodent · race ·

satellite · space · squirrel · seal · stripe · stitch · star · skunk · strawberry · snail · swan · sand castle ·

train · traveler · tapir · toothpaste · toothbrush · toucan · tulip · tomato · tortoise · track · toy · town · tent

unicorn · uniform · underwear · umbrella · up · unicycle · utensil · ukulele · underpass · upside down ·

volcano · vulture · valentine · village · volleyball · vitamin · viper · vine · vicuna · violet · vendor · vest ·

windmill · woodpecker · wishing well · window · web · watch · wagon · wood · walrus · whale · wedding ·

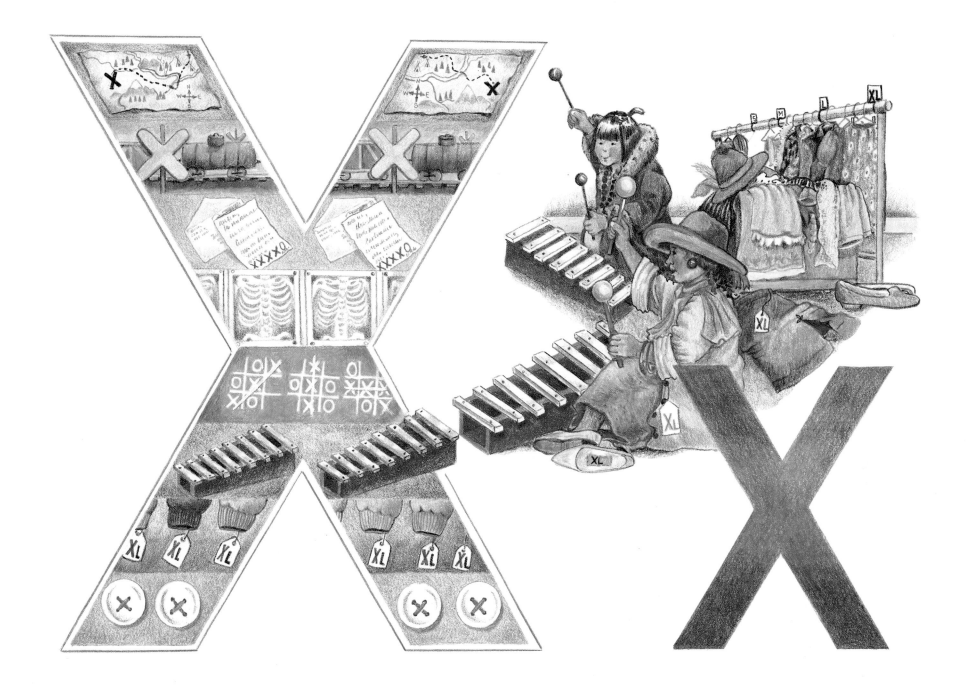

x marks the spot · railroad X-ing · x means kiss · X ray · x wins tic-tac-toe · xylophone · extra large ·

yellow · yo-yo · yarn · yacht · yoke · yellow jacket · yucca · yam · yurt · yak · yard · youngster · yawn ·

zeppelin · zither · zebra zone · zipper · zigzag · zebu · ziggurat · zinnia · zucchini · zebra · zzzzz ·

A B C D E F G H I J K L M N

anteater	embroidery	goose girl	heart	jade
antennae	eyelet	garbage	head	juggler
air	earring	garbage cans	hook	jar
	Easter egg	gnats	hut	jam
birdhouse	edelweiss	grain	hedge	jelly
beak	egret	gate	haystack	jester
buttonhole	easel	glove	hydrangea	jawbreaker
bush		grass	hollyhock	jigsaw puzzle
blackberry	fur	gingham	hyacinth	jug
	fin	goblet	hummingbird	
caravan	fireworks	glasses	heather	knitting
cannon	finger	grapefruit	hair	knothole
cactus	field	ground	hand	kimono
cowboy	farm	gravel	hermit	
circus	food	graph paper	hill	lake
	friend			lime
dust	fence		island	lamppost
dots	fern		iceberg	letter
darkness			ice skater	lamb
dachshund			igloo	leaf
dirt			iris	lightning
			ivy	lizard
			ice pick	lace
				ladybug

a b c d e f g h i j k l m n

O P Q R S T U V W X Y Z

O	P	R / Q	S	T / U / V	W / X / Y / Z
microphone	pod	Saturn	tepee	wash
moth	purple	snow	tunnel	wallpaper
medal	pink	seam	tree	wrist
mustache	puddle	sand	tower	wizard
	police officer	shovel	totem pole	witch
nestling	plaid	spoon	telephone pole	warthog
night	pigtail	scoop	tanker car	woods
notch	ponytail	shell	tender car	waterfall
name	pom-pom	sand dollar	trestle	winter
number	parka	sunglasses	trademark	wart
necklace	pennant	starfish		worm
nightlight	photo	sandpiper	Ursa Major	
nickel	pin	sailboat	Ursa Minor	x-stitch
		surf		
oxygen	quarters	sunset	villain	yardstick
orange	Queen Anne's lace	seashore	vegetable	yardage
oyster	quagmire		vase	
				zero
	racetrack			zoom lens
	runner			zoologist
	rag			
	railing			

o p q r s t u v w x y z

with thanks to Matt and Carrie

PUFFIN UNICORN BOOKS

Published by the Penguin Group
Penguin Books USA Inc., 375 Hudson Street,
New York, New York 10014, U.S.A.
Penguin Books Ltd, 27 Wrights Lane,
London W8 5TZ, England
Penguin Books Australia Ltd,
Ringwood, Victoria, Australia
Penguin Books Canada Ltd, 10 Alcorn Avenue,
Toronto, Ontario, Canada M4V 3B2
Penguin Books (N.Z.) Ltd, 182-190 Wairau Road,
Auckland 10, New Zealand
Penguin Books Ltd, Registered Offices:
Harmondsworth, Middlesex, England

Library of Congress number 89-1135
ISBN 0-14-055329-0

Published in the United States by
Dutton Children's Books,
a division of Penguin Books USA Inc.

Designer: Barbara Powderly
Printed in Hong Kong by
South China Printing Co.
First Puffin Unicorn Edition 1994
10 9 8 7 6 5 4 3 2 1

FROM LETTER TO LETTER is also available in
hardcover from Dutton Children's Books.